Pancakes with Mr. Bear

WRITTEN BY

Ryan Yackel

ART BY

Jordi Castells

Family time can be a challenge with all the hustle and bustle within our lives. And when we get family time, it's special and sacred.

Everyone wants to be a part of a family, and Mr. Bear is no different. I hope you enjoy this short story about a bear, pancakes, and family.

Ryan Yackel

For my girls, may always you seek out and
befriend those who want to be found.
-R.Y.

For Emilio and Remy, my little pancake lovers.
-J.C.

Once upon a time, there was a family who loved pancakes. Next to the family lived their grumpy neighbor, Mr. Bear.

While the family lived in a nice, cozy cottage, Mr. Bear lived in an old cabin near a gloomy mountain.

1

Every morning, the family would make a huge pancake breakfast. They tasted so good, and they smelled even better.

2

In fact, they smelled so wonderful that Mr. Bear
was reminded every day that he couldn't eat
them. This made Mr. Bear very angry.

But, no matter how hard he tried, Mr. Bear's pancakes always turned out tasting horrible.

5

One day Mr. Bear had enough of smelling his neighbor's wonderful pancakes. He threw open his cabin door and stomped all the way down the mountain toward their cozy cottage.

When Mr. Bear reached their front porch, he pounded on the door and growled,

Startled by Mr. Bear, Mommy opened the door and said, "I'm sorry, Mr. Bear, but we're having family time. If we have any pancakes left, I will leave them outside for you."

Mr. Bear wasn't happy and growled,

Then Daddy came to the door and said, "Mr. Bear, what if I give you one of my pancakes? Will that make you leave?"

Mr. Bear wasn't happy and growled,

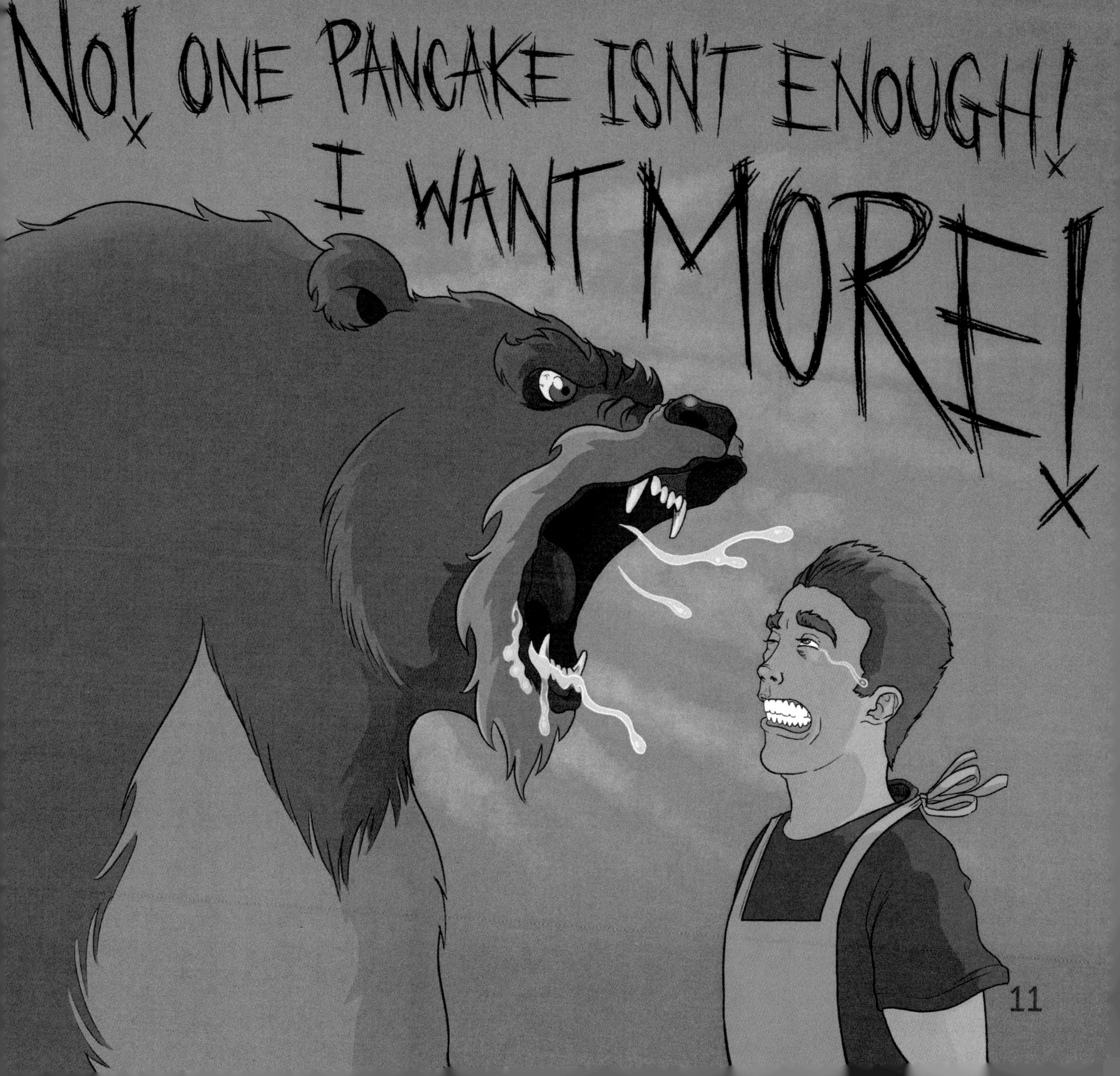

One of the little girls named Rosalie came to the door and said, "Mr. Bear, what if I give you five of my pancakes? Will that make you leave?"

Mr. Bear then became the angriest he's ever been and screamed,

No! No! Five Pancakes aren't Enough! I want the Pan-cakes! All

The youngest girl, named Winnie, came to the door and said, "Mr. Bear, I'm happy to give you all of my pancakes, but what I think you really want is a hug."

Mr. Bear began to open his mouth for a big roar but stopped. Just then, a little tear started to roll down his cheek. He looked at Winnie and said,

Yes, Winnie. That's exactly what I want.

Then Winnie gave Mr. Bear the biggest hug he'd ever had in his life. Rosalie, Daddy, and Mommy joined in to give Mr. Bear exactly what he wanted.

"Would you like to come in and have pancakes
with us, Mr. Bear?" the family asked.

"No thanks, I got what I came for," said Mr. Bear.

And with that warm hug, Mr. Bear walked back to his cabin.

17

The following morning, Winnie and Rosalie knocked on Mr. Bear's door.

"Would you like to join us for pancakes today?" the girls asked.

"Why yes, I would like that very much," smiled Mr. Bear.

"Guess what Mr. Bear?" Rosalie asked.

"What's that Rosalie?" smiled Mr. Bear.

"We're making blueberry pancakes today!"
Winnie cheered.

That morning, the family and Mr. Bear had one of the best pancake breakfasts ever. Mr. Bear's stomach got bigger with each bite and so did his heart.

You see, Mr. Bear got more than pancakes that morning. He got something better. He got a family.

The End

Made in the USA
Middletown, DE
03 December 2024

65974751R00015